BaD DoG

NiNa LadEn

Walker & Company ✹ New York

So they say I'm a bad dog.
I know I'm no Saint Bernard,
but it's not like I robbed a bank
or anything.
All I wanted to do
was have a little fun.
I was home.
Doing my job.
You know, watching things.
Watching the house.
Watching the squirrels outside.
Watching the TV.

I was bored.
Running on empty.
Empty water dish,
empty food bowl.
So I emptied the trash can.
That's when I found it.
My inspiration.
It was small and insignificant.
A postcard.
Just junk mail.
But to me it was an invitation.
A call of the wild.

On the front,
there was a photo of a farm.
On the back it said:

FREE-RANGE CHICKENS.

"Hallelujah," I howled,
"Farm fowls for free!"
Starving for adventure,
hungry for chicken,
I bolted out the dog door.
The fence was no obstacle.
I just thought of those luscious birds,
and winged it.
I was free.
The chickens were free.
"What a great world," I belted out
as I headed toward the freeway.

I was feeling good.
Unleashed and alive.
I jogged along,
stopping to smell the roses,
to roll in the grass,
to get down to earth.
I was digging my freedom.
I was pulling up roots.
All of a sudden
I was chased by a broom.
Swatted like a fly,
I flew into the road
where I almost caught a bus.
I escaped to the sidewalk,
looking for a way
to get to those chickens
without cooking my goose.
Then I remembered my buddy, Butch.

Butch worked at a gas station.

He had wheels.

He had fuel.

He was my ride.

I showed Butch the postcard.

He drooled all over it.

He showed me a car.

Heard his boss say it was a real dog.

"Perfect," I said,

"let's get rolling."

Butch fetched the key,

and cranked it up.

The car growled like a pit bull.

We roared off down the road.

Wind in our faces.

No one on our tails.

We were two happy dogs

looking for a free lunch.

We left the city.
We left the highway.
We took a left on a country road.
Everything seemed to be going right.
We took in the scenery.
We took in the sights.
We passed green fields,
yellow school buses
and red lights.
We were like two greyhounds
running a race.
Next thing we knew,
we were being chased.

Flashing lights were glaring.
Sirens were blaring.
We were being followed by police cars
in hot-dogged pursuit.
No one was going to beat us
to those chickens.
So we beat a path down the road.
We beat an oncoming train.
We didn't miss a beat.
The troopers were stopped dead
in their tracks.
And we rolled into the land of field,
farm, and free-range chickens.

Trailing a cloud of dust,
we homed in on our range.
There were farms on our left,
and farms on our right.
The air smelled
like a million paper-trained puppies.
Then I saw it.
The farm on the postcard.
It was better than beef on a bone.
A whole corral of chickens
all fattened up with no place to go.

Butch was beside himself,
and I was beside Butch.
A feast for the eyes
was there at our feet.
We savored the moment,
watching the soon-to-be
chicken fillets
and nuggets,
pot pies
and stews.
We could smell those chickens
roasting,
    grilling,
        broiling.
Our mouths were watering.
Our stomachs were
talking in tongues.

We were hungry.
We were greedy.
We licked our chops
and jumped into the pen.
At first, we tried to be friendly,
hoping the chickens we'd chosen
would come quietly.
We cornered a clucking cluster
and told them we were here to collect.
But they ignored us.
So we started barking orders.
We showed them we weren't chicken.
That's when things turned foul.

Chickens were squawking.
We were being henpecked
and picked at.
Feathers were flying.
Farmers came running.
Our free meal was a trap.
I told Butch to run.
He was chased by a dozen chickens,
pelted by a dozen eggs.
It was pure poultry in motion.
He flew the coop,
and I hunkered down,
tired and feathered.

I was in hot water.
Things were coming to a boil.
Farmers yelled,
"Get that poacher!"
"This won't be over easy,"
I mumbled as I scrambled to hatch a plan.
Suddenly, the police arrived.
They hollered,
"Take'im alive."
"Over my dead body,"
I growled.
"These chickens are mine."

With hens in tow,
I ran for the road.
An empty police car was running.
I counted my chickens,
and with eight wings and a prayer,
I jumped in the seat.
I gunned the engine
and shot off down the street.
The troopers were closing in.
So I opened the throttle.
"You're all a bunch of turkeys,"
I howled
as I led them on a wild goose chase.

Fortune was mine,
I thought.
But then I hit a bump in the road.
I lost control and razed a barn.
It was the end of my hayride.
The cops arrived.
They called me a robber.
They said I was wrong.
So they read me my rights.
Then they threw the book at me.
They took the chickens too.
I heard someone say
"they were going to fry."

I was locked up like a criminal,
waiting for my family
to come pay for me,
and for the free-range chickens
that I took.
After I was freed,
I saw a bucket of

fried chicken

in the next room.
"What a delicious twist of fate,"
I said.
Call me a "bad dog,"
but I got what I wanted.
And it was
finger-licking
good.

In homage to the Jacks: Jack Kerouac and Jack London

**Special thanks to Barbara Kouts for finding this dog a home,
and to Emily Easton for knowing a good bad dog when she sees one.**

First published in the United States of America in 2000 by Walker Publishing Company, Inc.

Published simultaneously in Canada by Fitzhenry and Whiteside, Markham, Ontario L3R 4T8

Library of Congress Cataloging-in-Publication Data

Laden, Nina.
    Bad dog / Nina Laden
        p.   cm
    Summary: A free-spirited, bored, and hungry dog misunderstands an ad for free range chickens, and when he and a friend set out to get some, they discover that the chickens— and the police—have other ideas.
    ISBN 0-8027-8747-9 (hardcover) — ISBN 0-8027-8748-7 (reinforced)
    [1. Dogs—Fiction. 2. Humorous stories.] I. Title.

PZ7.L13735 Bag 2000
[E]—dc21   00-024233

Book design by Sophie Ye Chin

Printed in Hong Kong

10 9 8 7 6 5 4 3 2